LITTLE WIZARD
Stories of
Oz

L. FRANK BAUM

Illustrated by
JOHN R. NEILL

Introduction by
MARTIN GARDNER

DOVER PUBLICATIONS, INC.
Mineola, New York

Copyright

Introduction copyright © 2011 by the Estate of Martin Gardner

Bibliographical Note

Little Wizard Stories of Oz, first published by Dover Publications, Inc., in 2011, is an unabridged republication of the work originally published by The Reilly & Britton Co., Chicago, in 1914. An Introduction has been written by Martin Gardner specially for the Dover edition.

Library of Congress Cataloging-in-Publication Data

Baum, L. Frank (Lyman Frank), 1856–1919.
 Little wizard stories of Oz / L. Frank Baum ; illustrated by John R. Neill ; introduction by Martin Gardner.
  p. cm.
 ISBN-13: 978-0-486-47644-5
 ISBN-10: 0-486-47644-8
 1. Children's stories, American. [1. Fantasy. 2. Short stories.] I. Neill, John R. (John Rea), ill. II. Title.

PZ7.B327Li 2011
[Fic]—dc22

2011004937

Manufactured in the United States by Courier Corporation
47644801
www.doverpublications.com

CONTENTS

INTRODUCTION

When Baker Street Irregulars speak of the "canon," the word has a precise meaning: It refers to the nine books about Sherlock Holmes written by Sir Arthur Conan Doyle (or should I say written by Dr. Watson?). It does not include the seemingly endless supply of novels and stories about Holmes written after Doyle died.

Oz scholars speak of the L. Frank Baum "canon," but now the word is less sharply defined. Does it, for example, include *Sea Fairies* and *Sky Island?* In both of those books all the action takes place outside Oz. This justifies leaving both books out of the canon. On the other hand, they are strongly tied to it. *Sea Fairies* introduces Trot and her peg-legged companion Cap'n Bill, both of whom later become Oz residents, and are featured in *The Scarecrow of Oz*. *Sky Island*, one of Baum's finest non-Oz fantasies, is about Trot, Cap'n Bill, and a Philadelphia boy named Button Bright. Button Bright appears in *The Road to Oz*, and also later becomes an Oz citizen. In *Sky Island*, the boy tells Trot that he has been to Oz. Both books are illustrated by John R. Neill, the Royal Illustrator of Oz. For all of these reasons, I would like to see *Sea Fairies* and *Sky Island* added to the Baum canon. I would also like to see *Little Wizard Stories of Oz* added to the Baum canon; all the stories are by Baum; all are illustrated by Neill; and all take place in Oz. They are delightfully written for children younger than readers of the canonical books, and they have a ring of authenticity not found in most Oz books not by Baum. Ruth Plumly Thompson has her deserved following, but essentially her twenty-one books are about an Oz not quite the same as Baum's. This also goes for later Oz books not written by Baum or Thompson, including four efforts by Neill (and one by me).

But enough about semantics. Let's take a look at the six Little Wizard Stories.

Neill's pictures here are among his best. Composition is superb, as are the colors added by the book's publisher. The book's first story is hilarious. Both the Cowardly Lion and Hungry Tiger express their desire to tear humans to pieces (the lion), and to eat fat little babies (the tiger). Of course, they don't mean what they say—It's all sham boasting. In a sense, they are humbugs like the Wizard before he learned real magic from Glinda. Both beasts, in spite of their wild talk, are harmless big cats with high moral principles. They speak of death, but we all know that in Oz no one dies (although they can be destroyed).

Neills first picture (see the frontispiece) is startling because it shows the lion of "The Cowardly Lion and the Hungry Tiger," the first story, wearing glasses! A comparison of the lion's eyes as seen through his spectacles to his eyes in other pictures show his eyes slightly enlarged by the convex lenses. This means that he is far-sighted, which in turn suggests that he likes to read and needs glasses for close-up vision.

In the book's second tale, "Little Dorothy and Toto," the mischievous Wizard, disguised as Crinklink, is teaching Dorothy the dangers of walking alone in Oz. It is hard to believe, but in Baum's initial draft of this chapter, Crinklink is an evil sorcerer who is finally, in his mouse-sized state, killed by Toto! Because people are seldom killed in Oz, Baum's publisher, Reilly and Britton, strongly objected to Toto's action. Baum agreed, and changed Crinklink to the Wizard. In my opinion, Baum's original ending was better than his later version. The Wizard's cruel joke on poor Dorothy seems completely out of character. I think children would have been delighted by Toto's destruction of Crinklink. On page 26 Baum makes a whopping mistake: He says that Toto, unlike the animals of Oz, is unable to speak. This error is understandable because it was not until he wrote *Tiktok of Oz*, a year after the Little Wizard stories, that Baum learned the truth about Toto. He could talk the moment he entered Oz. He just didn't want to!

After learning that Toto could speak, Dorothy, in *Tiktok of Oz*, struggles to persuade the dog to talk. All she gets are woofs. Finally, Toto blurts out, "All right, here I go!", and then dashes off in embarrassment. Toto talks a great deal in later Oz books. Millions of people who saw the Judy Garland film had, of course, no inkling that Toto could have a lot to say!

In the third Little Wizard story, "Tiktok and the Nome King," Baum correctly puts the Nome King in Ev, an enchanted land west of Oz, although he doesn't name the location. In this marvelous story about Tiktok we learn that in the Nome King's underground domain there is currency (in Oz there is no money), and that its unit is called a "specto."

In "Ozma and the Little Wizard," the fourth story, Neill failed to read Baum's text carefully. Baum says the imps have big ears and flat noses. Neill gives them tiny ears and projecting snouts. Baum's love of word play emerges in the strange names of the three imps. Each name, preceded by "imp," produces an adjective that describes an imp's constant behavior. Neill makes other blunders. On page 90, Ozma's dress has long sleeves. In earlier pictures the sleeves are short. And those birds on page 72 certainly are not doves—they look like hawks.

Jack Pumpkinhead's ability to obtain a new head after an old one spoils is featured in the fifth tale, "Jack Pumpkinhead and the Sawhorse." One thinks of other characters in Baum's Oz books who can change heads: Princess Langwidere (languid air) in *Ozma of Oz* has a cabinet filled with beautiful heads that she can wear at any time. In *The Tin Woodman of Oz*, the tin man has a disturbing conversation with his former head, which the tinsmith Ku-Klip has kept for years in a cupboard.

The black-and-white sketch heading page 97 shows Jack Curry combing the Sawhorse—this clearly is one of Neill's visual jokes. On the double-page spread on pages 100 to 101, Neill makes two mistakes: The text mentions a saddle, and states Jack sat in front with the children behind him. The picture shows no saddle and Jack is behind the children.

In the book's final chapter, "The Scarecrow and the Tin Woodman," we learn that the straw man's face is painted with watercolors, not oils. In his art on page 124 and 132 Neill remembers that Scarecrow's left eye is missing, but on pages 129 and 138 the left eye is mysteriously restored. We are told in this chapter that the Tin Woodman's heart is made of plush. This contradicts statements elsewhere in Baum's canon that the heart is made of silk velvet. We are also told that the pins and needles mixed with the bran in the Scarecrow's head make him sharp, repeating a pun by the Cowardly Lion in the first Oz book after the Wizard has given the straw man what he calls "bran-new" brains. Another Neill blunder is on page 120. The picture shows the boat's sail as white whereas we learn on page 127 that it is made out of purple silk.

Neill raises an interesting question on page 105. Jack always carves a new head with wide-open eyes, nose, and a broad grin. The picture shows a spoiled head with half-closed eyes and a frown. Can the pumpkin, when on Jack's neck, move his mouth and eyes? We can ask a similar question about the Scarecrow. Is he able to move his painted lips and close his painted eyes? In any case, Jack's old head clearly is not happy with having been discarded!

Michael Patrick Hearn, the author of *The Annotated Wizard of Oz*, probably knows more about Baum and Oz than anyone. Hearn reveals some truly startling information about three of the tales. Baum's original ending for "Little Dorothy and Toto" was, as I mentioned earlier, to have Toto attack Crinklink in his tiny form, the way a dog might attack a rat, and kill the evil sorcerer! "This is clearly away from your usual style of not doing any killing," wrote Sumner Britton, of Reilly and Britton Publishing. He made an amusing suggestion. "Why not," he asked, "have Crinklink grow larger again" and turn into the Wizard who is playing a joke on Dorothy? "Your suggestion is so excellent," Baum wrote back, "that I grabbed it straightaway."

Britton also objected to the word "ghost" in the tale about Tiktok. The word implies that Tiktok has a soul that can survive destruction of the body. But Tiktok is not alive. There is no way the Nome King could have imagined he was seeing Tiktok's ghost. Moreover, Britton said, the word "ghost" might frighten young readers. Again Baum agreed. As Hearn tells us, he wrote back, "All honor to the Great Baum who has made his machine man so real and life-like that even his publisher is horrified." Baum once more obliged by changing "ghost" to "phantom."

The third story Britton complained about was the final one. "It is sweet and pretty," he wrote, "yet it is not an astonishing tale the same as the other five." Baum accepted the criticism and wrote an entirely different chapter.

Neill borrowed some of his Little Wizard art for use in his next Oz book, *The Patchwork Girl of Oz*. The endpapers of *Little Wizard*, for example, are the endpapers of The *Patchwork Girl*, with Crinklink's castle in the background! Page 33 of *Little Wizard* shows Dorothy and Toto looking at a tiny Crinklink. The same picture appears meaninglessly in The *Patchwork Girl* with Crinklink missing and the dirt changed to a wood floor. Dorothy and Toto are staring at nothing!

Some of the pleasures of reading Baum's fantasies are the casual, wise remarks he slips into his narratives, such as his aside in the last chapter of this volume. The Scarecrow and Tin Woodman, we are told, are such good friends that they often separate so they can have the joy of meeting again!

And, finally, who is that man on page 28, behind a galloping horse, and why is he hurrying along a lonesome road that leads to Crinklink's castle?

MARTIN GARDNER
Norman, Oklahoma
August 2009

References

Paul R. Bienvenue and Robert E. Schmidt. *The Book Collector's Guide to L. Frank Baum*. March Hare Books, 2009. Pages 83–93.

David L. Greene. "The Little Wizard Stories: L. Frank Baum's Six Short Oz Books." The Baum Bugle, Vol. 17, Christmas 1973, page 19.

Michael Patrick Hearn. Introduction to *Little Wizard Stories of Oz* by L. Frank Baum. Schocken Books, 1985.

LITTLE WIZARD
Stories of
Oz

THE COWARDLY LION
and
THE HUNGRY TIGER

THE COWARDLY LION AND THE HUNGRY TIGER

N the splendid palace of the Emerald City, which is in the center of the fairy Land of Oz, is a great Throne Room, where Princess Ozma, the Ruler, for an hour each day sits in a throne of glistening emeralds and listens to all the troubles of her people, which they are sure to tell her about. Around Ozma's throne, on such occasions, are grouped all the important personages of Oz, such as the Scarecrow, Jack Pumpkinhead, Tiktok the Clockwork Man, the Tin Woodman, the Wizard of Oz, the

Shaggy Man and other famous fairy people. Little Dorothy usually has a seat at Ozma's feet, and crouched on either side the throne are two enormous beasts known as the Hungry Tiger and the Cowardly Lion.

These two beasts are Ozma's chief guardians, but as everyone loves the beautiful girl Princess there has never been any disturbance in the great Throne Room, or anything for the guardians to do but look fierce and solemn and keep quiet until the Royal Audience is over and the people go away to their homes.

Of course no one would dare be naughty while the huge Lion and Tiger crouched beside the throne; but the fact is, the people of Oz are very seldom naughty. So Ozma's big guards are more ornamental than useful, and no one realizes that better than the beasts themselves.

One day, after everybody had left the

Throne Room except the Cowardly Lion and the Hungry Tiger, the Lion yawned and said to his friend:

"I'm getting tired of this job. No one is afraid of us and no one pays any attention to us."

"That is true," replied the big Tiger, purring softly. "We might as well be in the thick jungles where we were born, as trying to protect Ozma when she needs no protection. And I'm dreadfully hungry all the time."

"You have enough to eat, I'm sure," said the Lion, swaying his tail slowly back and forth.

"Enough, perhaps; but not the kind of food I long for," answered the Tiger. "What I'm hungry for is fat babies. I have a great desire to eat a few fat babies. Then, perhaps, the people of Oz would fear me and I'd become more important."

"True," agreed the Lion. "It would stir up quite a rumpus if you ate but *one* fat baby. As for myself, my claws are sharp as needles and strong as crowbars, while my teeth are powerful enough to tear a person to pieces in a few seconds. If I should spring upon a man and make chop suey of him, there would be wild excitement in the Emerald City and the people would fall upon their knees and beg me for mercy. That, in my opinion, would render me of considerable importance."

"After you had torn the person to pieces, what would you do next?" asked the Tiger sleepily.

"Then I would roar so loudly it would shake the earth and stalk away to the jungle to hide myself, before anyone could attack me or kill me for what I had done."

"I see," nodded the Tiger. "You are really cowardly."

"To be sure. That is why I am named the Cowardly Lion. That is why I have always been so tame and peaceable. But I'm awfully tired of being tame," added the Lion, with a sigh, "and it would be fun to raise a row and show people what a terrible beast I really am."

The Tiger remained silent for several minutes, thinking deeply as he slowly washed his face with his left paw. Then he said:

"I'm getting old, and it would please me to eat at least one fat baby before I die. Suppose we surprise these people of Oz and prove our power. What do you say? We will walk out of here just as usual and the first baby we meet I'll eat in a jiffy, and the first man or woman you meet you will tear to pieces. Then we will both run out of the city gates and gallop

across the country and hide in the jungle before anyone can stop us."

"All right; I'm game," said the Lion, yawn-
ing again so that he showed two rows of dreadfully sharp teeth.

The Tiger got up and stretched his great,
sleek body.

"Come on," he said. The Lion stood up
and proved he was the larger of the two, for
he was almost as big as a small horse.

Out of the palace they walked, and met
no one. They passed through the beautiful
grounds, past fountains and beds of lovely
flowers, and met no one. Then they unlatched
a gate and entered street of the city, and met
no one.

"I wonder how a fat baby will taste," remarked the Tiger, as they stalked majestically
along, side by side.

"I imagine it will taste like nutmegs," said

the Lion.

"No," said the tiger, "I've an idea it will taste like gumdrops."

They turned a corner, but met no one, for the people of the Emerald City were accustomed to take their naps at this hour of the afternoon.

"I wonder how many pieces I ought to tear a person into," said the Lion, in a thoughtful voice.

"Sixty would be about right," suggested the Tiger.

"Would that hurt any more than to tear one into about a dozen pieces?" inquired the Lion, with a little shudder.

"Who cares whether it hurts or not?" growled the Tiger.

The Lion did not reply. They entered a side street, but met no one.

Suddenly they heard a child crying.

"Aha!" exclaimed the Tiger. "There is my meat."

He rushed around a corner, the Lion following, and came upon a nice fat baby sitting in the middle of the street and crying as if in great distress.

"What's the matter?" asked the Tiger, crouching before the baby.

"I—I—l—lost my m-m-mamma!" wailed the baby.

"Why, you poor little thing," said the great beast, softly stroking the child's head with its paw. "Don't cry, my dear, for mamma can't be far away and I'll help you to find her."

"Go on," said the Lion, who stood by.

"Go on where?" asked the Tiger, looking up.

"Go on and eat your fat baby."

"Why, you dreadful creature!" said the Tiger reproachfully; "would you want me to eat a poor little lost baby, that don't know

where its mother is?" And the beast gathered the little one into its strong, hairy arms
and tried to comfort it by rocking it gently
back and forth.

The Lion growled low in his throat and
seemed very much disappointed; but at that
moment a scream reached their ears and
a woman came bounding out of a house
and into the street. Seeing her baby in the
embrace of the monster Tiger the woman
screamed again and rushed forward to rescue
it, but in her haste she caught her foot in her
skirt and tumbled head over heels and heels
over head, stopping with such a bump that
she saw many stars in the heavens, although
it was broad daylight. And there she lay, in a
helpless manner, all tangled up and unable to
stir.

With one bound and a roar like thunder

the huge Lion was beside her. With his strong jaws he grasped her dress and raised her into an upright position.

"Poor thing! Are you hurt?" he gently asked.

Gasping for breath the woman struggled to free herself and tried to walk, but she limped badly and tumbled down again.

"My baby!" she said pleadingly.

"The baby is all right; don't worry," replied the Lion; and then he added: "Keep quiet, now, and I'll carry you back to your house, and the Hungry Tiger will carry your baby."

The Tiger, which had approached the place with the child in its arms, asked in astonishment:

"Aren't you going to tear her into sixty pieces?"

"No, nor into six pieces," answered the

Lion indignantly. "I'm not such a brute as to destroy a poor woman who has hurt herself trying to save her lost baby. If you are so ferocious and cruel and bloodthirsty, you may leave me and go away, for I do not care to associate with you."

"That's all right," answered the Tiger. "I'm not cruel—not in the least—I'm only hungry. But I thought *you* were cruel."

"Thank heaven I'm respectable," said the Lion, with dignity. He then raised the woman and with much gentleness carried her into her house, where he laid her upon a sofa. The tiger followed with the baby, which he safely deposited beside its mother. The little one liked the Hungry Tiger and grasping the enormous beast by both ears the baby kissed the beast's nose to show he was grateful and happy.

"Thank you very much," said the woman.

"I've often heard what good beasts you are, in spite of your power to do mischief to mankind, and now I know that the stories are true. I do not think either of you have ever had an evil thought."

The Hungry Tiger and the cowardly Lion hung their heads and did not look into each other's eyes, for both were shamed and humbled. They crept away and stalked back through the streets until they again entered the palace grounds, where they retreated to the pretty, comfortable rooms they occupied at the back of the palace. There they silently crouched in their usual corners to think over their recent adventure.

After a while the Tiger said sleepily:

"I don't believe fat babies taste like gumdrops. I'm quite sure they have the flavor of raspberry tarts. My, how hungry I am for fat babies!"

The Lion grunted disdainfully.

"You're a humbug," said he.

"Am I?" retorted the Tiger, with a sneer. "Tell me, then, into how many pieces you usually tear your victims, my bold Lion?"

The Lion impatiently thumped the floor with his tail.

"To tear anyone into pieces would soil my claws and blunt my teeth," he said. "I'm glad I didn't muss myself up this afternoon by hurting that poor mother."

The Tiger looked at him steadily and then yawned a wide, wide yawn.

"You're a coward," he remarked.

"Well," said the Lion, "it's better to be a coward than to do wrong."

"To be sure," answered the other. "And that reminds me that I nearly lost my own reputation. For, had I eaten that fat baby, I would not now be the Hungry Tiger. It's better to go hungry, seems to me, than to be cruel to a little child."

And then they dropped their heads on their paws and went to sleep.

LITTLE DOROTHY
and
TOTO

LITTLE DOROTHY AND TOTO

OROTHY was a little Kansas girl who once accidentally found the beautiful Land of Oz and was invited to live there always. Toto was Dorothy's small black dog, with fuzzy, curly hair and bright black eyes. Together, when they tired of the grandeur of the Emerald City of Oz, they would wander out into the country and all through the land, peering into queer nooks and corners and having a good time in their own simple way. There was a little Wizard living in Oz who was a faithful friend of

Dorothy and did not approve of her traveling alone in this way, but the girl always laughed at the little man's fears for her and said she was not afraid of anything that might happen.

One day, while on such a journey, Dorothy and Toto found themselves among the wild wooded hills at the southeast of Oz—a place usually avoided by travelers because so many magical things abounded there. And, as they entered a forest path, the little girl noticed a sign tacked to a tree, which said: "Look out for Crinklink."

Toto could not talk, as many of the animals of Oz can, for he was just a common Kansas dog; but he looked at the sign so seriously that Dorothy almost believed he could read it, and she knew quite well that Toto understood every word she said to him.

"Never mind Crinklink," said she. "I don't believe anything in Oz will try to hurt us,

Toto, and if I get into trouble you must take care of me."

"Bow-wow!" said Toto, and Dorothy knew that meant a promise.

The path was narrow and wound here and there between the trees, but they could not lose their way, because thick vines and creepers shut them in on both sides. They had walked a long time when, suddenly turning a curve of the pathway, they came upon a lake of black water, so big and so deep that they were forced to stop.

"Well, Toto," said Dorothy, looking at the lake, "we must turn back, I guess, for there is neither a bridge nor a boat to take us across the black water."

"Here's the ferryman, though," cried a tiny voice beside them, and the girl gave a start and looked down at her feet, where a man no taller than three inches sat at the edge of the path with his legs dangling over the lake.

"Oh!" said Dorothy; "I didn't see you before."

Toto growled fiercely and made his ears stand up straight, but the little man did not seem in the least afraid of the dog. He merely repeated: "I'm the ferryman, and it's my business to carry people across the lake."

Dorothy couldn't help feeling surprised, for she could have picked the little man up with one hand, and the lake was big and broad. Looking at the ferryman more closely she saw that he had small eyes, a big nose and a sharp chin. His hair was blue and his clothes scarlet, and Dorothy noticed that every button on his jacket was the head of some animal. The top button was a bear's head and

the next button a wolf's head; the next was a cat's head and the next a weasel's head, while the last button of all was the head of a field-mouse. When Dorothy looked into the eyes of these animals' heads, they all nodded and said in a chorus: "Don't believe all you hear, little girl!"

"Silence!" said the small ferryman, slapping each button head in turn, but not hard enough to hurt them. Then he turned to Dorothy and asked: "Do you wish to cross over the lake?"

"Why, I'd like to," she answered, hesitating; "but I can't see how you will manage to carry us, without any boat."

"If you can't see, you mustn't see," he answered with a laugh. "All you need do is shut your eyes, say the word, and—over you go!"

Dorothy wanted to get across, in order that she might continue her journey.

"All right," she said, closing her eyes; "I'm ready."

Instantly she was seized in a pair of strong arms—arms so big and powerful that she was startled and cried out in fear.

"Silence!" roared a great voice, and the girl opened her eyes to find that the tiny man had suddenly grown to a giant and was holding both her and Toto in a tight embrace while in one step he spanned the lake and reached the other shore.

Dorothy became frightened, then, especially as the giant did not stop but continued tramping in great steps over the wooded hills, crushing bushes and trees beneath his broad feet. She struggled in vain to free herself, while Toto whined and trembled beside her, for the little dog was frightened, too.

"Stop!" screamed the girl. "Let me down!" But the giant paid no attention. "Who are

you, and where are you taking me?" she continued; but the giant said not a word. Close to Dorothy's ear, however, a voice answered her, saying: "This is the terrible Crinklink, and he has you in his power."

Dorothy managed to twist her head around and found it was the second button on the jacket—the wolf's head—which had spoken to her.

"What will Crinklink do with me?" she asked anxiously.

"No one knows. You must wait and see," replied the wolf.

"Some of his captives he whips," squeaked the weasel's head.

"Some he transforms into bugs, and other things," growled the bear's head.

"Some he enchants, so that they become doorknobs," sighed the cat's head.

"Some he makes his slaves—even as we

are—and that is the most dreadful fate of all," added the field-mouse. "As long as Crinklink exists we shall remain buttons, but as there are no more buttonholes on his jacket he will probably make you a slave."

Dorothy began to wish she had not met Crinklink. Meantime, the giant took such big steps that he soon reached the heart of the hills, where, perched upon the highest peak, stood a log castle. Before this castle he paused to set down Dorothy and Toto, for Crinklink was at present far too large to enter his own doorway. So he made himself grow smaller, until he was about the size of an ordinary man. Then he said to Dorothy, in stern, commanding tones:

"Enter, girl!"

Dorothy obeyed and entered the castle, with Toto at her heels. She found the place to be merely one big room. There was a table

and chair of ordinary size near the center, and
at one side a wee bed that seemed scarcely big
enough for a doll. Everywhere else were dishes—dishes—dishes! They were all soiled, and
were piled upon the floor, in all the corners
and upon every shelf. Evidently Crinklink
hadn't washed a dish for years, but had cast
them aside as he used them.

Dorothy's captor sat down in the chair and
frowned at her.

"You are young and strong, and will make
a good dishwasher," said he.

"Do you mean me to wash all those
dishes?" she asked, feeling both indignant
and fearful, for such a task would take weeks
to accomplish.

"That's just what I mean," he retorted. "I
need clean dishes, for all I have are soiled,
and you're going to make 'em clean or get
trounced. So get to work and be careful not to

break anything. If you smash a dish, the penalty is one lash from my dreadful cat-o'-nine-tails for every piece the dish breaks into," and here Crinklink displayed a terrible whip that made the little girl shudder.

Dorothy knew how to wash dishes, but she remembered that often she carelessly broke one. In this case, however, a good deal depended on being careful, so she handled the dishes very cautiously.

While she worked, Toto sat by the hearth and growled low at Crinklink, and Crinklink sat in his chair and growled at Dorothy because she moved so slowly. He expected her to break a dish any minute, but as the hours passed away and this did not happen Crinklink began to grow sleepy. It was tiresome watching the girl wash dishes and often he glanced longingly at the tiny bed. Now he began to yawn, and he yawned and yawned until

finally he said:

"I'm going to take a nap. But the buttons on my jacket will be wide awake and whenever you break a dish the crash will waken me. As I'm rather sleepy I hope you won't interrupt my nap by breaking anything for a long time."

Then Crinklink made himself grow smaller and smaller until he was three inches high and of a size to fit the tiny bed. At once he lay down and fell fast asleep.

Dorothy came close to the buttons and whispered: "Would you really warn Crinklink if I tried to escape?"

"You can't escape," growled the bear. "Crinklink would become a giant, and soon overtake you."

"But you might kill him, while he sleeps," suggested the cat, in a soft voice.

"Oh!" cried Dorothy, drawing back; "I

couldn't poss'bly *kill* anything—even to save
my life."

But Toto had heard this conversation and
was not so particular about killing monsters.
Also the little dog knew he must try to save
his mistress. In an instant he sprang upon the
wee bed and was about to seize the sleeping
Crinklink in his jaws when Dorothy heard a
loud crash and a heap of dishes fell from the
table to the floor. Then the girl saw Toto and
the little man rolling on the floor together,
like a fuzzy ball, and when the ball stopped
rolling, behold! there was Toto wagging his
tail joyfully and there sat the little Wizard of
Oz, laughing merrily at the expression of surprise on Dorothy's face.

"Yes, my dear, it's me," said he, "and I've
been playing tricks on you—for your own
good. I wanted to prove to you that it is really
dangerous for a little girl to wander alone in a

fairy country; so I took the form of Crinklink to teach you a lesson. There isn't any Crink-link, to be sure; but if there had been you'd be severely whipped for breaking all those dishes."

The Wizard now rose, took off the coat with the button heads, and spread it on the floor, wrong side up. At once there crept from beneath it a bear, a wolf, a cat, a weasel and a field-mouse, who all rushed from the room and escaped into the mountains.

"Come on, Toto," said Dorothy; "let's go back to the Emerald City. You've given me a good scare, Wizard," she added, with dignity, "and p'raps I'll forgive you, by'n'by; but just now I'm mad to think how easily you fooled me."

TIKTOK
and
THE NOME KING

TIKTOK AND THE NOME KING

 HE Nome King was unpleasantly angry. He had carelessly bitten his tongue at breakfast and it still hurt; so he roared and raved and stamped around in his underground palace in a way that rendered him very disagreeable.

It so happened that on this unfortunate day Tiktok, the Clockwork Man, visited the Nome King to ask a favor. Tiktok lived in the Land of Oz and although he was an active and important person, he was made entirely of metal. Machinery within him, something like the works of a clock, made him move; other machinery made him talk; still other machinery made him think.

Although so cleverly constructed, the Clockwork Man was far from perfect. Three separate keys wound up his motion machinery, his speech works and his thoughts. One or more of these contrivances was likely to run down at a critical moment, leaving poor Tiktok helpless. Also some of his parts were wearing out, through much use, and just now his thought machinery needed repair. The skillfull little Wizard of Oz had tinkered with Tiktok's thoughts without being able to get them properly regulated, so he had advised the Clockwork Man to go to the Nome King and secure a new set of springs, which would render his thoughts more elastic and responsive.

"Be careful what you say to the Nome King," warned the Wizard. "He has a bad temper and the least little thing makes him angry."

Tiktok promised, and the Wizard wound his machinery and set him walking in the direction of the Nome King's dominions, just across the desert from the Land of Oz. He ran down just as he reached the entrance to the underground palace, and there Kaliko, the Nome King's Chief Steward, found him and wound him up again.

"I want to see the King," said Tiktok, in his jerky voice.

"Well," remarked Kaliko, "it may be safe for a cast-iron person like you to face his Majesty this morning; but you must announce yourself, for should I show my face inside the jewel-studded cavern where the King is now raving, I'd soon look like a dish of mashed potatoes, and be of no further use to anyone."

"I'm not a-fraid," said Tiktok.

"Then walk in and make yourself at home," answered Kaliko, and threw open the door of the King's cavern.

Tiktok promptly walked in and faced the astonished Nome King, to whom he said: "Good morn-ing. I want two new steel springs for my thought-works and a new cog-wheel for my speech-pro-du-cer. How a-bout it, your Maj-es-ty?"

The Nome King growled a menacing growl and his eyes were red with rage.

"How dare you enter my presence?" he shouted.

"I dare an-y-thing," said Tiktok. "I'm not a-fraid of a fat Nome."

This was true, yet an unwise speech. Had Tiktok's thoughts been in good working or-der he would have said something else. The

angry Nome King quickly caught up his heavy
mace and hurled it straight at Tiktok. When
it struck the metal man's breast, the force of
the blow burst the bolts which held the plates
of his body together and they clattered to the
floor in a score of pieces. Hundreds and hundreds of wheels, pins, cogs and springs filled
the air like a cloud and then rattled like hail
upon the floor.

Where Tiktok had stood was now only
a scrap-heap and the Nome King was so
amazed by the terrible effect of his blow that
he stared in wonder.

His Majesty's anger quickly cooled. He remembered that the Clockwork Man was a favorite subject of the powerful Princess, Ozma
of Oz, who would be sure to resent Tiktok's
ruin.

"Too bad!" too bad!" he muttered, regret-
fully. "I'm really sorry I made junk of the fel-

low. I didn't know he'd break."

"You'd better be," remarked Kaliko, who now ventured to enter the room. "You'll have a war on your hands when Ozma hears of this, and the chances are you will lose your throne and your kingdom."

The Nome King turned pale, for he loved to rule the Nomes and did not know of any other way to earn a living in case Ozma fought and conquered him.

"Do—do you think Ozma will be angry?" he asked anxiously.

"I'm sure of it," said Kaliko. "And she has the right to be. You've made scrap-iron of her favorite."

The King groaned.

"Sweep him up and throw the rubbish into the black pit," he commanded; and then he shut himself up in his private den and for days would see no one, because he was so ashamed

of his unreasoning anger and so feared the results of his rash act.

Kaliko swept up the pieces, but he did not throw them into the black pit. Being a clever and skillful mechanic he determined to fit the pieces together again.

No man ever faced a greater puzzle; but it was interesting work and Kaliko succeeded. When he found a spring or wheel worn or imperfect, he made a new one. Within two weeks, by working steadily night and day, the Chief Steward completed his task and put the three sets of clockworks and the last rivet into Tiktok's body. He then wound up the motion machinery and the Clockwork Man walked up and down the room as naturally as ever. Then Kaliko wound up the thought works and the speech regulator and said to Tiktok:

"How do you feel now?"

"Fine," said the Clockwork Man. "You have

done a ve-ry good job, Kal-i-ko, and saved me from de-struc-tion. Much o-bliged."

"Don't mention it," replied the Chief Steward. "I quite enjoyed the work."

Just then the Nome King's gong sounded and Kaliko rushed away through the jewel-studded cavern and into the den where the King had hidden, leaving the doors ajar.

"Kaliko," said the King, in a meek voice, "I've been shut up here long enough to repent bitterly the destruction of Tiktok. Of course Ozma will have revenge, and send an army to fight us, but we must take our medicine. One thing comforts me; Tiktok wasn't really a live person; he was only a machine man, and so it wasn't very wicked to stop his clockworks. I couldn't sleep nights, at first, for worry; but there's no more harm in smashing a machine man than in breaking a wax doll. Don't you think so?"

"I am too humble to think in the presence of your Majesty," said Kaliko.

"Then get me something to eat," commanded the King, "for I'm nearly starved. Two roasted goats, a barrel of cakes and nine mince pies will do me until dinnertime."

Kaliko bowed and hurried away to the royal kitchen, forgetting Tiktok, who was wandering around in the outer cavern. Suddenly the Nome King looked up and saw the Clockwork Man standing before him, and at the sight the monarch's eyes grew big and round and he fell a-trembling in every limb.

"Away, grim Shadow!" he cried, "You're not here, you know; you're only a hash of cogwheels and springs, lying at the bottom of the black pit. Vanish, thou Vision of the demolished Tiktok, and leave me in peace—for I have bitterly repented!"

"Then beg my pardon," said Tiktok in a

gruff voice, for Kaliko had forgotten to oil the speech works.

But the sound of a voice coming from what he thought a mere vision was too much for the Nome King's shaken nerves. He gave a yell of fear and rushed from the room. Tiktok followed, so the King bolted through the corridors on a swift run and bumped against Kaliko, who was returning with a tray of things to eat. The sound of the breaking dishes, as they struck the floor, added to the King's terror and he yelled again and dashed into a great cavern where a thousand Nomes were at work hammering metal.

"Look out!" Here comes a phantom clockwork man!" screamed the terrified monarch, and every Nome dropped his tools and made a rush from the cavern, knocking over their King in their mad flight and recklessly trampling upon his prostrate fat body. So, when

Tiktok came into the cavern, there was only the Nome King left, and he was rolling upon the rocky floor and howling for mercy, with his eyes fast shut so that he could not see what he was sure was a dreadful phantom that was coming straight toward him.

"It oc-curs to me," said Tiktok calmly, "that your Maj-es-ty is act-ing like ba-by. I am not a phan-tom. A phan-tom is un-real, while I am the real thing."

The King rolled over, sat up and opened his eyes.

"Didn't I smash you to pieces?" he asked in trembling tones.

"Yes," said Tiktok.

"Then you are nothing but a junk-heap, and this form in which you now appear can-not be real."

"It is, though," declared Tiktok. "Kali-ko picked up my piec-es and put me togeth-er a-gain. I'm as good as new, and perhaps bet-ter."

"That is true, your Majesty," added Kaliko, who now made his appearance," and I hope you will forgive me for mending Tiktok. He was quite broken up, after you smashed him, and I found it almost as hard a job to match his pieces as to pick turnips from gooseberry bushes. But I did it," he added proudly.

"You are forgiven," announced the Nome King, rising to his feet and drawing a long breath. "I will raise your wages one specto a year, and Tiktok shall return to the Land of Oz loaded with jewels for the Princess Ozma."

"That is all right," said Tiktok. "But what I want to know is, why did you hit me with your mace?"

"Because I was angry," admitted the King. "When I am angry I always do some-thing that I am sorry for afterward. So I have

firmly resolved never to get angry again; unless—unless—"

"Unless what, your Majesty?" inquired Kaliko.

"Unless something annoys me," said the Nome King. And then he went to his treasure-chamber to get the jewels for Princess Ozma of Oz.

Ozma
and
The Little Wizard

OZMA AND THE LITTLE WIZARD

NCE upon a time there lived in the beautiful Emerald City, which lies in the center of the fairy Land of Oz, a lovely girl called Princess Ozma, who was Ruler of all that country. And among those who served this girlish Ruler and lived in a cosy suite of rooms in her splendid palace, was a little, withered old man known as the Wizard of Oz.

This little Wizard could do a good many queer things in magic; but he was a kind man, with merry, twinkling eyes and a sweet smile; so, instead of fearing him because of his magic, everybody loved him.

Now, Ozma was very anxious that all her people who inhabited the pleasant Land of Oz should be happy and contented, and therefore she decided one morning to make a journey to all parts of the country, that she might discover if anything was amiss, or anyone discontented, or if there was any wrong that ought to be righted. She asked the little Wizard to accompany her and he was glad to go.

"Shall I take my bag of magic tools with me?" he asked.

"Of course," said Ozma. "We may need a lot of magic before we return, for we are going into strange corners of the land, where we may meet with unknown creatures and dangerous adventures."

So the Wizard took his bag of magic tools

and the two left the Emerald City and wandered over the country for many days, at last reaching a place far up in the mountains which neither of them had ever visited before. Stopping one morning at a cottage, built beside the rocky path which led into a pretty valley beyond, Ozma asked a man:

"Are you happy? Have you any complaint to make of your lot?"

And the man replied:

"We are happy except for three mischievous Imps that live in yonder valley and often come here to annoy us. If your Highness would only drive away those Imps, I and my family would be very happy and very grateful to you."

"Who are these bad Imps?" inquired the girl Ruler.

"One is named Olite, and one Udent and one Ertinent, and they have no respect for anyone or anything. If strangers pass through the valley the Imps jeer at them and make horrid faces and call names, and often they push travelers out of the path or throw stones at them. Whenever Imp Olite or Imp Udent or Imp Ertinent comes here to bother us, I and my family run into the house and lock all the doors and windows, and we dare not venture out again until the Imps have gone away."

Princess Ozma was grieved to hear this report and the little Wizard shook his head gravely and said the naughty Imps deserved to be punished. They told the good man they would see what could be done to protect him and at once entered the valley to seek the dwelling place of the three mischievous creatures.

Before long they came upon three caves, hollowed from the rocks, and in front of

each cave squatted a queer little dwarf. Ozma and the Wizard paused to examine them and found them well-shaped, strong and lively. They had big round ears, flat noses and wide grinning mouths, and their jet-black hair came to points on top of their heads, much resembling horns. Their clothing fitted snugly to their bodies and limbs and the Imps were so small in size that at first Ozma did not consider them at all dangerous. But one of them suddenly reached out a hand and caught the dress of the Princess, jerking it so sharply that she nearly fell down, and a moment later another Imp pushed the little Wizard so hard that he bumped against Ozma and both unexpectedly sat down upon the ground.

At this the Imps laughed boisterously and began running around in a circle and kicking dust upon the Royal Princess, who cried in a sharp voice: "Wizard, do your duty!"

The Wizard promptly obeyed. Without rising from the ground he opened his bag, got the tools he required and muttered a magic spell.

Instantly the three Imps became three bushes—of a thorny, stubby kind—with their roots in the ground. As the bushes were at first motionless, perhaps through surprise at their sudden transformation, the Wizard and the Princess found time to rise from the ground and brush the dust off their pretty clothes. Then Ozma turned to the bushes and said:

"The unhappy lot you now endure, my poor Imps, is due entirely to your naughty actions. You can no longer annoy harmless travelers and you must remain ugly bushes, covered with sharp thorns, until you repent of your bad ways and promise to be good Imps."

"They can't help being good, now, your

Highness," said the Wizard, who was much pleased with his work, "and the safest plan will be to allow them always to remain bushes."

But something must have been wrong with the Wizard's magic, or the creatures had magic of their own, for no sooner were the works spoken than the bushes began to move. At first they only waved their branches at the girl and the little man, but pretty soon they began to slide over the ground, their roots dragging through the earth, and one pushed itself against the Wizard and pricked him so sharply with its thorns that he cried out: "Ouch!' and started to run away.

Ozma followed, for the other bushes were trying to stick their thorns into her legs and one actually got so near her that it tore a great rent in her beautiful dress. The girl Princess could run, however, and she followed the fleeing Wizard until he tumbled head first over a log and rolled upon the ground. Then she sprang behind a tree and shouted: "Quick! Transform them into something else."

The Wizard heard, but he was much confused by his fall. Grabbing from his bag the first magical tool he could find he transformed the bushes into three white pigs. That astonished the Imps. In the shape of pigs—fat, roly-poly and cute—they scampered off a little distance and sat down to think about their new condition.

Ozma drew a long breath and coming from behind the tree she said:

"That is much better, Wiz, for such pigs as these must be quite harmless. No one need now fear the mischievous Imps."

"I intended to transform them into mice," replied the Wizard, "but in my excitement I worked the wrong magic. However, unless the

horrid creatures behave themselves hereafter, they are liable to be killed and eaten. They would make good chops, sausages or roasts."

But the Imps were now angry and had no intention of behaving. As Ozma and the little Wizard turned to resume their journey the three pigs rushed forward, dashed between their legs and tripped them up, so that both lost their balance and toppled over, clinging to one another. As the Wizard tried to get up he was tripped again and fell across the back of the third pig, which carried him on a run far down the valley until it dumped the little man into the river. Ozma had been sprawled upon the ground but found she was not hurt, so she picked herself up and ran to the assistance of the Wizard, reaching him just as he was crawling out of the river, gasping for breath and dripping with water. The girl could not help laughing at his woeful appearance. But he had no sooner wiped the wet from his eyes than one of the impish pigs tripped him again and sent him into the river for a second bath. The pigs tried to trip Ozma, too, but she ran around a stump and so managed to keep out of their way. So the Wizard scrambled out of the water again and picked up a sharp stick to defend himself. Then he mumbled a magic mutter which instantly dried his clothes, after which he hurried to assist Ozma. The pigs were afraid of the sharp stick and kept away from it.

"This won't do," said the Princess. "We have accomplished nothing, for the pig Imps would annoy travelers as much as the real Imps. Transform them into something else, Wiz."

The Wizard took time to think. Then he transformed the white pigs into three blue doves.

"Doves," said he, "are the most harmless things in the world."

But scarcely had he spoken when the doves flew at them and tried to peck out their eyes. When they endeavored to shield their eyes with their hands two of the doves bit the Wizard's fingers and another caught the pretty pink ear of the Princess in its bill and gave it such a cruel tweak that she cried out in pain and threw her skirt over her head.

"These birds are worse then the pigs, Wizard," she called to her companion. "Nothing is harmless that is animated by impudent anger or impertinent mischief. You must transform the Imps into something that is not alive."

The Wizard was pretty busy, just then, driving off the birds, but he managed to open his bag of magic and find a charm which instantly transformed the doves into three buttons. As they fell to the ground he picked them up and smiled with satisfaction. The tin button was Imp Olite, the brass button was Imp Udent and the lead button was Imp Ertinent. These buttons the Wizard placed in a little box which he put in his jacket pocket. "Now," said he, "the Imps cannot annoy travelers, for we shall carry them back with us to the Emerald City."

But we dare not use the buttons," said Ozma, smiling once more now that the danger was over.

"Why not?" asked the Wizard. "I intend to sew them upon my coat and watch them carefully. The spirits of the Imps are still in the buttons, and after a time they will repent and be sorry for their naughtiness. Then they will decide to be very good in the future. When they feel that way, the tin button will turn to silver and the brass to gold, while the lead

button will become aluminum. I shall then restore them to their proper forms, changing their names to pretty names instead of the ugly ones they used to bear. Thereafter the three Imps will become good citizens of the Land of Oz and I think you will find they will prove faithful subjects of our beloved Princess Ozma."

"Ah that is magic well worth while," exclaimed Ozma, well pleased. "There is no doubt, my friend, but that you are a very clever Wizard."

Jack Pumpkinhead
and
The Sawhorse

JACK PUMPKINHEAD AND
THE SAWHORSE.

I N a room of the Royal Palace of the Emerald City of Oz hangs a Magic Picture, in which are shown all the important scenes that transpire in those fairy dominions. The scenes shift constantly, and by watching them, Ozma, the girl Ruler, is able to discover events taking place in any part of her kingdom.

One day she saw in her Magic Picture that a little girl and a little boy had wandered together into a great, gloomy forest at the far

97

west of Oz and had become hopelessly lost. Their friends were seeking them in the wrong direction and unless Ozma came to their rescue the little ones would never be found in time to save them from starving.

So the Princess sent a message to Jack Pumpkinhead and asked him to come to the Palace. This personage, one of the queerest of the queer inhabitants of Oz, was an old friend and companion of Ozma. His form was made of rough sticks fitted together and dressed in ordinary clothes. His head was a pumpkin with a face carved upon it, and was set on top a sharp stake which formed his neck.

Jack was active, good-natured and a general favorite; but his pumpkin head was likely to spoil with age, so in order to secure a good supply of heads he grew a big field of pumpkins and lived in the middle of it, his house

being a huge pumpkin hollowed out. Whenever he needed a new head he picked a pumpkin, carved a face on it and stuck it upon the stake of his neck, throwing away the old head as of no further use.

The day Ozma sent for him Jack was in prime condition and was glad to be of service in rescuing the lost children. Ozma made him a map, showing just where the forest was and how to get to it and the paths he must take to reach the little ones. Then she said:

"You'd better ride the Sawhorse, for he is swift and intelligent and will help you accomplish your task."

"All right," answered Jack, and went to the royal stable to tell the Sawhorse to be ready for the trip.

This remarkable animal was not unlike Jack Pumpkinhead in form, although so different in shape. Its body was a log, with four sticks stuck into it for legs. A branch at one end of the log served as a tail, while in the other end was chopped a gash that formed a mouth. Above this were two small knots that did nicely for eyes. The Sawhorse was the favorite steed of Ozma and to prevent its wooden legs from wearing out she had them shod with plates of gold.

Jack said "Good morning" to the Sawhorse and placed upon the creature's back a saddle of purple leather, studded with jewels.

"Where now?" asked the horse, blinking its knot eyes at Jack.

"We're going to rescue two babes in the wood," was the reply. Then he climbed into the saddle and the wooden animal pranced out of the stable, through the streets of the Emerald City and out upon the highway leading to the western forest where the children were lost.

Small though he was, the Sawhorse was swift and untiring. By nightfall they were in the far west and quite close to the forest they sought. They passed the night standing quietly by the roadside. They needed no food, for their wooden bodies never became hungry; nor did they sleep, because they never tired. At daybreak they continued their journey and soon reached the forest.

Jack now examined the map Ozma had given him and found the right path to take, which the Sawhorse obediently followed. Underneath the trees all was silent and gloomy and Jack beguiled the way by whistling gayly as the Sawhorse trotted along.

The paths branched so many times and in so many different ways that the Pumpkinhead was often obliged to consult Ozma's map, and finally the Sawhorse became suspicious.

"Are you sure you are right?" it asked.

"Of course," answered Jack. "Even a Pumpkinhead whose brains are seeds can follow so clear a map as this. Every path is plainly marked, and here is a cross where the children are."

Finally they reached a place, in the very heart of the forest, where they came upon the lost boy and girl. But they found the two children bound fast to the trunk of a big tree, at the foot of which they were sitting.

When the rescuers arrived, the little girl was sobbing bitterly and the boy was trying to comfort her, though he was probably frightened as much as she.

"Cheer up, my dears," said Jack, getting out of the saddle. "I have come to take you back to your parents But why are you bound to that tree?"

"Because," cried a small, sharp voice, "they are thieves and robbers. That's why!"

"Dear me!" said Jack, looking around to see who had spoken. The voice seemed to come from above.

A big gray squirrel was sitting upon a low branch of the tree. Upon the squirrel's head was a circle of gold, with a diamond set in the center of it. He was running up and down the limbs and chattering excitedly.

"These children," continued the squirrel, angrily, "robbed our storehouse of all the nuts we had saved up for the winter. There-fore, being the King of all the Squirrels in this forest, I ordered them arrested and put in prison, as you now see them. They had no right to steal our provisions and we are going to punish them."

"We were hungry," said the boy, plead-ingly, "and we found a hollow tree full of nuts, and ate them to keep alive. We didn't want to starve when there was food right in front of us."

"Quite right," remarked Jack, nodding his pumpkin head. "I don't blame you one bit, under the circumstances. Not a bit."

Then he began to untie the ropes that bound the children to the tree.

"Stop that!" cried the King Squirrel, chattering and whisking about. "You mustn't release our prisoners. You have no right to."

But Jack paid no attention to the protest. His wooden fingers were awkward and it took him some time to untie the ropes. When at last he succeeded, the tree was full of squirrels, called together by their King, and they were furious at losing their prisoners. From the tree they began to hurl nuts at the Pumpkinhead, who laughed at them as he helped the two children to their feet.

Now, at the top of this tree was a big dead limb, and so many squirrels gathered upon it that suddenly it broke away and fell to the ground. Poor Jack was standing directly under it and when the limb struck him it smashed his pumpkin head into a pulpy mass and sent Jack's wooden form tumbling, to stop with a bump against a tree a dozen feet away.

He sat up, a moment afterward, but when he felt for his head it was gone. He could not see; neither could he speak. It was perhaps the greatest misfortune that could have happened to Jack Pumpkinhead, and the squirrels were delighted. They danced around in the tree in great glee as they saw Jack's plight.

The boy and girl were indeed free, but their protector was ruined. The Sawhorse was there, however, and in his way he was wise. He had seen the accident and knew that the smashed pumpkin would never again serve

Jack as a head. So he said to the children, who were frightened at this accident to their new found friend.

"Pick up the Pumpkinhead's body and set it on my saddle. Then mount behind it and hold it on. We must get out of this forest as soon as we can, or the squirrels may capture you again. I must guess at the right path, for Jack's map is no longer of any use to him since that limb destroyed his head."

The two children lifted Jack's body, which was not at all heavy, and placed it upon the saddle. Then they climbed up behind it and the Sawhorse immediately turned and trotted back along the path he had come, bearing all three with ease. However, when the path began to branch into many paths, all following different directions, the wooden animal became puzzled and soon was wandering aimlessly about, without any hope of finding the

right way. Toward evening they came upon a fine fruit tree, which furnished the children a supper, and at night the little ones lay upon a bed of leaves while the Sawhorse stood watch, with the limp, headless form of poor Jack Pumpkinhead lying helpless across the saddle.

Now, Ozma had seen in her Magic Picture all that had happened in the forest, so she sent the little Wizard, mounted upon the Cowardly Lion, to save the unfortunates. The Lion knew the forest well and when he reached it he bounded straight through the tangled paths to where the Sawhorse was wandering, with Jack and the two children on his back.

The Wizard was grieved at the sight of the headless Jack, but believed he could save him. He first led the Sawhorse out of the forest and restored the boy and girl to the arms of their anxious friends, and then he sent the Lion back to Ozma to tell her what had happened.

The Wizard now mounted the Sawhorse and supported Jack's form on the long ride to the pumpkin field. When they arrived at Jack's house the Wizard selected a fine pumpkin—not too ripe—and very neatly carved a face on it. Then he stuck the pumpkin solidly on Jack's neck and asked him:

"Well, old friend, how do you feel?"

"Fine!" replied Jack, and shook the hand of the little Wizard gratefully. "You have really saved my life, for without your assistance I could not have found my way home to get a new head. But I'm all right, now, and I shall be very careful not to get this beautiful head smashed." And he shook the Wizard's hand again.

"Are the brains in the new head any better than the old ones?" inquired the Sawhorse,

who had watched Jack's restoration.

"Why, these seeds are quite tender," replied the Wizard, "so they will give our friend tender thoughts, But, to speak truly, my dear Sawhorse, Jack Pumpkinhead, with all his good qualities, will never be noted for his wisdom.

The Scarecrow
and
The Tin Woodman

THE SCARECROW AND THE
TIN WOODMAN

THERE lived in the Land of Oz two queerly made men who were the best of friends. They were so much happier when together that they were seldom apart; yet they liked to separate, once in awhile, that they might enjoy the pleasure of meeting again.

One was a Scarecrow. That means he was a suit of blue Munchkin clothes, stuffed with straw, on top of which was fastened a round cloth head, filled with bran to hold it in shape.

On the head were painted two eyes, two ears, a nose and a mouth. The Scarecrows had never been much of a success in scaring crows, but he prided himself on being a superior man, because he could feel no pain, was never tired and did not have to eat or drink. His brains were sharp, for the Wizard of Oz had put pins and needles in the Scarecrow's brain.

The other man was made all of tin, his arms and legs and head being cleverly jointed so that he could move them freely. He was known as the Tin Woodman, having at one time been a woodchopper, and everyone loved him because the Wizard had given him an excellent heart of red plush.

The Tin Woodman lived in a magnificent tin castle, built on his country estate in the Winkie Land, not far from the Emerald City of Oz. It had pretty tin furniture and was surrounded by lovely gardens in which were

many tin trees and beds of tin flowers. The palace of the Scarecrow was not far distant, on the banks of a river, and this palace was in the shape of an immense ear of corn.

One morning the Tin Woodman went to visit his friend the Scarecrow, and as they had nothing better to do they decided to take a boat ride on the river. So they got into the Scarecrow's boat, which was formed from a big corncob, hollowed out and pointed at both ends and decorated around the edges with brilliant jewels. The sail was of purple silk and glittered gayly in the sunshine.

There was a good breeze that day, so the boat glided swiftly over the water. By and by they came to a smaller river that flowed from out a deep forest, and the Tin Woodman proposed they sail up this stream, as it would be cool and shady beneath the trees of the forest. So the Scarecrow, who was steering, turned the boat up the stream and the friends continued talking together of old times and the wonderful adventures they had met with while traveling with Dorothy, the little Kansas girl. They became so much interested in this talk that they forgot to notice that the boat was now sailing through the forest, or that the stream was growing more narrow and crooked.

Suddenly the Scarecrow glanced up and saw a big rock just ahead of them.

"Look out!" he cried; but the warning came too late.

The Tin Woodman sprang to his feet just as the boat bumped into the rock, and the jar made him lose his balance. He toppled and fell overboard and being made of tin he sank to the bottom of the water in an instant and lay there at full length, face up.

Immediately the Scarecrow threw out the

anchor, so as to hold the boat in that place, and then he leaned over the side and through the clear water looked at his friend sorrowfully.

"Dear me!" he exclaimed; "what a misfortune."

"It is, indeed," replied the Tin Woodman, speaking in muffled tones because so much water covered him. "I cannot drown, of course, but I must lie here until you find a way to get me out. Meantime, the water is soaking into all my joints and I shall become badly rusted before I am rescued."

"Very true," agreed the Scarecrow; "but be patient, my friend, and I'll dive down and get you. My straw will not rust, and is easily replaced, if damaged, so I'm not afraid of the water."

The Scarecrow now took off his hat and made a dive from the boat into the water; but he was so light in weight that he barely dented the surface of the stream, nor could he reach the Tin Woodman with his outstretched straw arms. So he floated to the boat and climbed into it, saying the while:

"Do not despair, my friend. We have an extra anchor aboard, and I will tie it around my waist, to make me sink, and dive again."

"Don't do that!" called the tin man. "That would anchor you also to the bottom, where I am, and we'd both be helpless."

"True enough," signed the Scarecrow, wiping his wet face with a handkerchief; and then he gave a cry of astonishment, for he found he had wiped off one painted eye and now had but one eye to see with.

"How dreadful!" said the poor Scarecrow. "That eye must have been painted in watercolor, instead of oil. I must be careful not to wipe off the other eye, for then I could not

see to help you at all."

A shriek of elfish laughter greeted this speech and looking up the Scarecrow found the trees full of black crows, who seemed much amused by the straw man's one-eyed countenance. He knew the crows well, however, and they had usually been friendly to him because he had never deceived them into thinking he was a meat man—the sort of man they really feared.

"Don't laugh," said he; "you may lose an eye yourselves, some day."

We couldn't look as funny as you, if we did," replied one old crow, the king of them. "But what has gone wrong with you?"

"The Tin Woodman, my dear friend and companion, has fallen overboard and is now on the bottom of the river," said the Scarecrow. "I'm trying to get him out again, but I fear I shall not succeed."

"Why, it's easy enough," declared the old crow. "Tie a string to him and all of my crows will fly down, take hold of the string, and pull him up out of the water. There are hundreds of us here, so our united strength could lift much more than that."

"But I can't tie a string to him," replied the Scarecrow. "My straw is so light that I am unable to dive through the water. I've tried it, and knocked one eye out."

"Can't you fish for him?"

"Ah, that is a good idea," said the Scarecrow. "I'll make the attempt."

He found a fishline in the boat, with a stout hook at the end of it. No bait was needed, so the Scarecrow dropped the hook into the water till it touched the Woodman.

"Hook it into a joint," advised the crow, who was now perched upon a branch that stuck far out and bent down over the water.

The Scarecrow tried to do this, but having only one eye he could not see the joints very clearly.

Hurry up, please," begged the Tin Wood-man; "you've no idea how damp it is down here."

"Can't you help" asked the crow.

"How?" inquired the Tin Man.

"Catch the line and hook it around your neck."

The Tin Woodman made the attempt and after several trials wound the line around his neck and hooked it securely.

"Good!" cried the King Crow, a mischievous old fellow. "Now, then, we'll all grab the line and pull you out."

At once the air was filled with black crows, each of whom seized the cord with beak or talons. The Scarecrow watched them with much interest and forgot that he had tied the other end of the line around his own waist, so he would not lose it while fishing for his friend.

"All together for the good caws!" shrieked the King Crow, and with a great flapping of wings the birds rose into the air.

The Scarecrow clapped his stuffed hands in glee as he saw his friend drawn from the water into the air; but next moment the straw man was himself in the air, his stuffed legs kicking wildly; for the crows had flown straight up through the trees. On one end of the line dangled the Tin Woodman, hung by the neck, and on the other dangled the Scarecrow, hung by the waist and clinging fast to the spare anchor of the boat, which he had seized hoping to save himself.

"Hi, there—be careful!" shouted the Scarecrow to the crows. "Don't take us so high. Land us on the river bank."

But the crows were bent on mischief. They thought it a good joke to bother the two, now that they held them captive.

"Here's where the crows scare the Scarecrow!" chuckled the naughty King Crow, and at his command the birds flew over the forest to where a tall dead tree stood higher than all the other trees. At the very top was a crotch, formed by two dead limbs, and into the crotch the crows dropped the center of the line. Then, letting go their hold, they flew away, chattering with laughter, and left the two friends suspended high in the air—one on each side the tree.

Now the Tin Woodman was much heavier than the Scarecrow, but the reason they balanced so nicely was because the straw man still clung fast to the iron anchor. There they hung, not ten feet apart, yet unable to reach the bare tree-trunk.

"For goodness sake don't drop that anchor," said the Tin Woodman anxiously.

"Why not?" inquired the Scarecrow.

"If you did I'd tumble to the ground, where my tin would be badly dented by the fall. Also you would shoot into the air and alight somewhere among the tree-tops."

"Then," said the Scarecrow, earnestly, "I shall hold fast to the anchor."

For a time they both dangled in silence, the breeze swaying them gently to and fro. Finally the tin man said: "Here is an emergency friend, where only brains can help us. We must think of some way to escape."

"I'll do the thinking," replied the Scarecrow. "My brains are the sharpest."

He thought so long that the tin man grew tired and tried to change his position, but found his joints had already rusted so badly that he could not move them. And his oil-can

was back in the boat.

"Do you suppose your brains are rusted, friend Scarecrow?" he asked in a weak voice, for his jaws would scarcely move.

"No, indeed. Ah, here's an idea at last!"

With this the Scarecrow clapped his hands to his head, forgetting the anchor, which tumbled to the ground. The result was astonishing; for, just as the Tin Man had said, the light Scarecrow flew into the air, sailed over the top of the tree and landed in a bramble-bush, while the tin man fell plump to the ground, and landing on a bed of dry leaves was not dented at all. The Tin Woodman's joints were so rusted, however, that he was unable to move, while the thorns held the Scarecrow a fast prisoner.

While they were in this sad plight the sound of hoofs was heard and along the forest path rode the little Wizard of Oz, seated on a wooden Sawhorse, He smiled when he saw the one-eyed head of the Scarecrow sticking out of the bramble-bush, but he helped the poor straw man out of his prison.

"Thank you, dear Wiz," said the grateful Scarecrow. "Now we must get the oil-can and rescue the Tin Woodman."

Together they ran to the river bank, but the boat was floating in midstream and the Wizard was obliged to mumble some magic words to draw it to the bank, so the Scarecrow could get the oil-can. Then back they flew to the tin man, and while the Scarecrow carefully oiled each joint the little Wizard moved the joints gently back and forth until they worked freely. After an hour of this labor the Tin Woodman was again on his feet, and although still a little stiff he managed to walk to the boat.

The Wizard and the Sawhorse also got

aboard the corncob craft and together they returned to the Scarecrow's palace. But the Tin Woodman was very careful not to stand up in the boat again.